SUPER HEROES

BATMAN AND SUPERMAN SWAPPED!

By **Richard Ashley Hamilton**

Random House 🏠 **New York**

Manufactured under license granted to AMEET Sp. z o.o.
by the LEGO Group.

AMEET Sp. z o.o.
Nowe Sady 6, 94–102 Łódź—Poland
ameet@ameet.eu
www.ameet.eu

www.LEGO.com

Published in the United States by Random House Children's Books, a division of
Penguin Random House LLC, 1745 Broadway, New York, NY 10019, and in Canada by
Penguin Random House Canada Limited, Toronto. Random House and the colophon
are registered trademarks of Penguin Random House LLC.

Visit us on the Web!
rhcbooks.com

ISBN 978-0-593-57090-6 (trade) — ISBN 978-0-593-57091-3 (lib. bdg.)
ISBN 978-0-593-57092-0 (ebook)

MANUFACTURED IN CHINA

10 9 8 7 6 5 4 3 2 1

First Edition 2023

CONTENTS

CHARACTER PROFILES:

Mr. Mxyzptlk
This magical imp loves to prank Super Heroes. The only way to stop Mr. Mxyzptlk is to make him say his name backward—but he may have an extra trick under his hat this time.

Superman
Superman was born on the planet Krypton, then adopted by a loving couple on Earth. Today he defends truth and justice for all as a reporter named Clark Kent—and the superpowered Man of Steel.

Batman
After a tragic robbery left young Bruce Wayne an orphan, he dedicated his mind and body to fighting crime. The Batman now uses his intelligence, gadgets, and vehicles to keep Gotham City safe for all.

The Anti-Monitor

In our universe, there is only one Earth. But in the multiverse, there are many Earths—and the Anti-Monitor will stop at nothing to destroy all of them, triggering a Crisis on Infinite Earths.

Cyborg

When a lab accident gravely wounded his body, Victor Stone was rebuilt with cutting-edge technology, making him a half-man/half-machine hero. Cyborg may be covered in metal, but he is full of heart.

Darkseid

Darkseid rules the war-torn world of Apokolips with a stone fist and his destructive Omega Beams! But controlling one planet isn't enough, so he now targets Earth and the Super Heroes who protect it.

Parademons

The shock troops in Darkseid's Apokolips army, Parademons are like overgrown insects—they wear armored exoskeletons, fly in swarms, and destroy everything in their path. A big can of bug spray won't stop them, but the Justice League can!

Alfred

Alfred the butler raised young Bruce Wayne as if the boy were his own son. Now that the boy has grown into Batman, Alfred still cares for the Caped Crusader by building his Bat-gadgets!

Robin

Robin isn't just Batman's sidekick—he's also Batman's friend. The Boy Wonder uses his smarts to foil Super-Villains and his fun-loving sense of adventure to bring a little lightheartedness to the Dark Knight Detective.

Batgirl

Batgirl, a martial artist and computer genius, is one of Batman's partners. She solves mysteries and stops crime, whether in her uniform or in her secret identity of Barbara Gordon.

Granny Goodness

A formidable warrior who trains every soldier in Darkseid's army, Granny Goodness is a lot like her world of Apokolips—rough, tough, and as hot-tempered as the planet's blazing fire pits.

Kalibak

Darkseid's big brute of a son, Kalibak only wants his fearsome father's approval, even though he secretly possesses something Darkseid does not: compassion. Maybe Kalibak isn't such a chip off the old blockhead after all.

Chapter 1
What's the Anti-Matter?

The weather forecast in the *Daily Planet* for Monday morning in Metropolis called for cool temperatures, scattered clouds, and a slight chance of rain. Instead, the city experienced red skies, anti-matter showers, and an invasion of evil shadows.

"Yep, it's a Monday, all right," said Superman, as he soared over his city, slaloming between swirling portals, the mysterious openings to

another dimension. Dozens of dark shadow beings poured out of each portal, but their leader—and Superman's main target—loomed ahead.

The Anti-Monitor, a super powerful adversary clad in armor who had once already tried to destroy the known universe, towered over the Metropolis skyline. His giant hands had built an equally giant machine on top of a high-rise building, and strange, crackling energy surged from it. Far below, people fled in terror.

"ADMIT DEFEAT, KRYPTONIAN," the Anti-Monitor's voice boomed. "SOON THIS ANTI-MATTER UNIT SHALL CONVERT YOUR DIMENSION INTO MY NEW HOME!"

Before Superman could answer, another voice, low and gravelly, said, "Uninvited guests are like fish—they stink after a few days."

Batman flew his Batwing right under the Anti-Monitor's nose—well, the space where his nose *would* be if he had one. Superman sidled up to Batman's sleek jet. "Nice of you to swing by," he said.

"I would have gotten here sooner, but there was turbulence over Blüdhaven," Batman explained. "Those weather forecasts between Gotham City and New Jersey are never right."

Superman rocketed toward the Anti-Monitor, but the interdimensional invader swatted the

hero away. The Man of Steel plummeted to the ground, sliding for several blocks. Shadow beings clung to the Batwing, trying to pry away its stealth shielding like gremlins. But Batman flew his jet in a loop-de-loop, shaking off the creepy creatures just as Superman launched himself back into the air.

"I assume you have a plan in mind?" Superman asked.

"Always," answered Batman. "*You* box the shadows; I'll pull the plug."

"You know, Batman, you'll make more friends if you say 'please,'" Superman suggested.

"I have enough friends," said Batman. "Now get to work. *Please.*"

Superman smiled, but that smile faded when he spotted a tree below him. A kitten was stuck on the highest branch, shivering as the trunk swayed in the anti-matter storm and more shadow beings gathered nearby. Superman squared his shoulders. "First things first," he said.

He swooped down and took the kitten into his arms a split-second before the topmost branch snapped. The rescued kitten purred in relief, and Superman scratched her chin as he blew away the shadow beings with his super-breath. More shadow beings closed in—only to disintegrate when a bright light struck them! The Batwing streaked past, Batman's portable Bat-Signal shining from the top of it.

"Even when surrounded by a shadow squadron, you *still* find the time to save a cat," said Batman as he landed his aircraft on the street. "No wonder people call you the Big Blue Boy Scout."

"They do?" asked Superman as he landed with the kitten.

"I'll have Alfred sew a merit badge onto your cape," Batman replied.

As he exited his vehicle, the kitten hissed at Batman. "Eh, I'm more of a dog person anyway," he said.

There was a rumbling sound overhead—and beneath the Super Heroes' boots. Superman's super-hearing instantly told him that the sound wasn't thunder. Soon the rumbling came from all around them. Deep cracks spread up and down the streets and on the sides of buildings. Whole chunks of pavement and concrete broke off and flew toward the Anti-Monitor's machine. Powerful turbines vacuumed the chunks into one end, while the other end churned out deadly anti-matter. The Anti-Monitor then drank in this eerie energy and grew *even bigger*!

"I've heard of energy drinks, but this is ridiculous!" said Superman.

"Stick to the plan," said Batman.

Superman set the kitten safely on the ground, then picked up the Bat-Signal as if it were as weightless as a tuft of cotton candy. He took to the air, aiming the Bat-Signal like a spotlight and blowing up the new wave of shadow beings.

With the brilliant light show drawing the Anti-Monitor's attention, Batman crept closer to the anti-matter machine. The Caped Crusader was accustomed to the darkness of Gotham, not the sunny streets of this city. But as he turned a corner, a Metropolis man raced by screaming, "Run for your life!"

"Now I feel like I'm at home," Batman said.

High above him, the sky reddened with another influx of anti-matter. Time was running out. Batman fired his grappling hook, which snagged a nearby building and drew him upward. Landing on the rooftop, Batman approached the Anti-Monitor's machine.

"STAY AWAY FROM THAT!" the Anti-Monitor shouted.

"You didn't say 'please,'" Batman said.

It was time to pull the plug on the machine. Batman spotted some wires trailing out of it and gave a mighty yank, triggering a spray of sparks and smoke.

"NO!" bellowed the Anti-Monitor, swinging his huge fist, about to pulverize Batman.

But something flashed in the Anti-Monitor's eyes. Batman had just enough time to tuck and roll out of the way before the Anti-Monitor's fist slammed down, accidentally smashing his own device. The portals began closing, and the shadow beings quickly retreated into them. Only the last vortex—the big one through which the Anti-Monitor had invaded—remained.

"NOOOO!" the Anti-Monitor cried again.

Dusting off his cape, Batman saw that Superman was keeping the Bat-Signal's bright beam fixed on the Anti-Monitor's face, forcing him backward. After a few stumbling steps, the Anti-Monitor's enormous foot caught on the Batwing. He fell into his own portal, which shrank into a tiny black pinprick before closing forever.

"And stay out," said Batman.

Superman landed beside him, returning the Bat-Signal to the Batwing. "Thanks for the assist, friend," he said. "Can you stay for coffee?"

"Can't," Batman said curtly. "Caffeine makes me cranky."

They grinned and shook hands—just before everything changed completely.

A pulsing glare, far harsher than the Bat-Signal, lit up Metropolis. When it faded, the laws of gravity had flipped. Superman and Batman watched in alarm as clouds sank to the ground. Cars drifted up to the sky, their drivers jumping out just as the tires left the roads. Even the hefty spinning globe on top of the Daily Planet Building floated away like a hot-air balloon!

But none of that compared to the most startling change of all. Batman and Superman discovered that their uniforms also swapped! Now Clark Kent wore the Batsuit, while Bruce Wayne found himself in the Superman's red, blue, and yellow uniform. The switch startled the kitten, who jumped back into the same tree, her fur standing on end.

"Great Krypton!" Superman said under Batman's cowl.

"There's nothing great about this," Batman growled, covering his exposed face.

To protect his secret identity, Batman hastily removed his mask from Superman's head and put it back where it belonged. But when they tried to exchange the rest of their uniforms,

not a single article of clothing would budge, as if the garments were magnetized to their bodies.

"This is some serious static cling!" Superman said. "Looks like we're stuck in each other's suits—at least until we figure out what went wrong with gravity."

"Everything that's supposed to be up is down, and everything that's supposed to be down is up," said Batman. "But this inverted gravity affects only inanimate objects, not living things. It doesn't make sense!"

"Maybe not," giggled a high-pitched voice as a floating imp in a purple bowler hat magically appeared, but it sure is fun!"

Chapter 2
You Can't Spell "Mxyzptlk" Without the "Why"

"I just flew in from the Fifth Dimension, and, boy, are my arms tired!" Mr. Mxyzptlk—a Super-Villain who was small in stature but big on buffoonery—laughed so hard at his own joke, he almost lost his hat. Wiping away a tear, he sauntered past the mixed-up Superman and Batman and found a cloud that had settled on the sidewalk. With a snap of his fingers, the cumulus molded into a comfortable lounge seat. Mxyzptlk even pulled a cloud lever and comfortably propped his feet on an extending footrest!

"Seriously, though, it sure was grand of the Anti-Monitor to attack this dimension," the reclining imp said. "If he hadn't opened those portals, I couldn't have sneaked through!"

Superman had dealt with Mxyzptlk's antics several times in the past, with each encounter leaving the hero both exhausted and annoyed.

"We have to get Mxyzptlk to say his name backward," he whispered to Batman. "It's the only way to stop him, and—"

Superman's voice trailed off. He grew concerned. "Wait. If Mxyzptlk can make clouds fall from the sky—then what about airplanes?" he said.

Mxyzptlk broke into shrill laughter again, and Batman felt a headache coming on. His vision went blurry before it snapped into clear focus. Batman's eyes saw farther than ever before, like twin telescopes. He spotted a LexAir cargo plane plummeting toward the earth!

"Incoming!" Batman shouted.

Superman squinted in the direction where Batman was pointing, but, strangely enough, he didn't see anything. Nevertheless, the Man of Steel leapt into the air, saying, "This looks like a job for Super—"

To his utter surprise, instead of rocketing up to the sky, Superman fell flat on his face. Mr. Mxyzptlk doubled over laughing.

Batman saw his Batwing floating away with every other parked vehicle and bounded

toward it. Amazingly, Batman's jump took him so high off the ground, he nearly overshot the Batwing! Batman managed to grab a wing, climb inside his jet, and stomp on the gas pedal—but his foot punched straight through the bottom of the hull as if it were made of paper.

"Whoops!" said Mxyzptlk. "I'm so sorry! Did I forget to mention I swapped your superpowers?"

"Batman!" Superman said, when he finally spotted the falling cargo plane. "You need to fly! I'll teach you. Just clear your mind!"

Batman had some difficulty doing that, with the cargo plane sinking like a stone. But then he noticed the gentle pull of air currents over, under, and around his body.

"It . . . tickles," Batman said. "I don't like being tickled."

Superman cheered. "That means it's working!" he said. "Keep it up!"

Channeling those invisible tides, Batman concentrated . . . concentrated . . . and floated off the Batwing! But Batman wasn't the world's most graceful flyer. His backside was higher than his shoulders, and his red cape draped over his head.

"No one in the League can ever hear about this!" barked Batman.

Despite his ungainly start, Batman straightened out. He picked up speed, streamlining his body to reduce wind resistance. Superman then remembered the grappling hook in Batman's Utility Belt. He aimed it at Batman's red cape, which had been *his* red cape only moments before, and fired, hoping to hitch a ride. But Superman miscalculated, and the hook broke against Batman's hard head.

Batman finally, fitfully reached the front of the plane and righted it, using his newfound strength to slow the nosediving aircraft. On the other side of the windshield, two grateful

pilots waved at Superman—at least, they *thought* it was Superman, but . . . in a Batman mask?

As the pilots blinked in confusion, the plane's rear large cargo door malfunctioned. It swung wide open, and several bags of feathers, pillows, and biodegradable packing peanuts spilled out.

"Traveling light, I see!" Batman quipped while bracing the plane on his back.

Hundreds of feet below, Superman saw the plunging cargo. With Mxyzptlk's inverted gravity, even lightweight materials would do untold damage if they collided with the ground at that velocity. Superman latched another grappling hook onto the rudderless Batwing. The line retracted, drawing him to the jet's control panel, where he flipped a switch. A crash foam cannon at the front of the Batwing swiveled out. Superman had seen Batman use it before and knew he'd have to gauge his shot just right. The cargo kept changing course as it whistled through the wind, blowing this way and that. If Superman fired foam at one spot too early, and the cargo wound up making impact somewhere else, the crater would be big enough to swallow Metropolis. The cargo hurtled ever closer, going from one hundred feet away to fifty feet to five!

At the last second, Superman fired the cannon, discharging gallons of crash foam—a white goop that expanded and thickened, looking like a huge marshmallow. The feathers, pillows, and packing peanuts hit it dead center, bull's-eye, then sank into the insulated foam, safe and sound. A moment later, Batman eased the plane onto the street, and the pilots evacuated down an inflatable yellow slide.

"Bravo!" applauded Mr. Mxyzptlk from his cloud lounger.

"Why, Mxyzptlk?" Superman said. "Your swap is putting innocent lives at stake!"

"Because the confusion will only speed up *my* takeover of your dimension!" the imp said. "The Anti-Monitor isn't the only one who wanted a change of scenery, after all! And that's my cue to bid you adieu!"

The teasing trickster disappeared with another laugh, leaving the Super Heroes with mismatched suits, mismatched powers, and many, many questions.

Chapter 3
Watch Out!

Batman started to get the hang of flying—
and Superman found himself strangely out
of breath—as they finished securing every
loose object in the city. Countless Batropes
tethered formerly heavy objects like, trains
and park fountains, while grounded drones
and helicopters littered the streets.

"I think I need . . . a nap?" Superman said
wearily.

"We should head to the Watchtower to see the full extent of Mxyzptlk's swapping spell," said Batman.

Superman nodded, lifting his arms to fly. When nothing happened, he said, "Oh . . . right."

"Don't worry," Batman said. "We'll figure it out."

He put an arm around Superman and carried him back to the Batwing, then lifted the entire aircraft into the sky. Superman watched through the bulletproof windshield as they left Metropolis, then North America, then Earth's atmosphere. It was a view Superman had enjoyed thousands of times before—but never as a passenger. He sighed, and Batman's vastly improved hearing picked up on the sound.

"Something got you down?" asked the Caped Crusader.

"Other than gravity, you mean?" the Man of Steel quipped. "I guess I'm just feeling kind of . . . powerless as a regular human. Er, no offense!"

"None taken," said Batman, who was surprised to learn that he really *wasn't* offended.

In fact, the Dark Knight felt an emotion quite unfamiliar to him—happiness. It had taken him some time to process these new abilities. But now Batman started to imagine what his one-man war on crime would look like with powers. Why, with his super-hearing, he'd be able to eavesdrop on The Penguin's scheming. He'd solidify that slippery scoundrel, Clayface, with super-breath. He could even use super-speed to defuse The Joker's exploding jack-in-the-boxes before they could spring!

"Now the joke will be on *you*, Joker!" Batman said out loud.

"Huh?" a preoccupied Superman said.

"Um, I just used your super-vision to check on that kitten," Batman fibbed. "She's fine."

"That's good to hear," Superman said.

Yet the last son of Krypton experienced a heaviness in his heart, just as the rest of his body seemed heavy without the gift of flight. Superman felt disappointed, although not for himself. He worried what Mxyzptlk's magic meant for Metropolis. How would Superman be able to protect his friends, like Lois Lane and Jimmy Olsen, and the hundreds of thousands of other citizens?

Superman shook his head to clear the troubling thoughts. After all, he may have been born on Krypton, but he'd been raised in Smallville, Kansas. And Ma and Pa Kent didn't bring up their only boy to feel sorry for himself. The memory of his adoptive parents cheered Superman as they reached the Watchtower, the Justice League's space station.

Sunlight reflected off the gleaming satellite headquarters, a titanic construct of steel and glass locked in geosynchronous orbit with the Earth. Wide panels collected solar energy, which was used to power the Watchtower. Batman's enhanced sight scoped the open hangar doors at the lower tier of the base.

"Activating landing gear now," announced Superman.

He saw a switch marked L.G. and flipped it—ejecting two missiles from the Batwing, which struck the Watchtower!

"I don't get it!" Superman exclaimed. "I pushed the L.G. button!"

Batman pinched the space between his eyes and said, "That stands for 'launch grenades'. You wanted the button that says D.U.—'deploy undercarriage.'"

The Caped Crusader had expected his fellow hero to say he was sorry—Superman often did, even for unintentional mishaps—but no apology came. Not that it mattered much at this moment, as the blasted part of the Watchtower broke off from the rest of the satellite.

"I'll fuse it back together with my heat vision—er, *your* heat vision," said Batman.

He felt a burning sensation start to build up behind his corneas. Then two searing beams lasered out of them. But instead of welding the broken segment back onto the Watchtower, the beams accidentally sheared off a completely different section!

"Uh-oh," Superman and Batman said at the same time.

All of a sudden, every light in the Batwing blinked repeatedly, as if pairing with another device. Then the jet went into autopilot and nimbly approached the Watchtower's hangar.

"Are you doing this?" Superman asked.

"I thought *you* were!" said Batman.

"Actually, I think you've both done *more* than enough for now," said a third voice.

The two Super Heroes looked back toward the headquarters and saw their teammate, Cyborg, repairing the damage they had caused. While his internal computers remotely controlled the Batwing, the half-man/half-machine hero transformed his hands into an electromagnet and proton blaster. The magnet attracted the debris to the satellite, and the positively charged particles soldered it securely in place.

"There," said Cyborg. "No harm, no foul. I'm just glad I was on monitor duty!"

Batman and Superman arrived inside the hangar with the Batwing. Cyborg prepared to join them, but something briefly registered on his highly attuned internal sensors. He scanned the space around him, yet saw nothing on any of the visible or invisible spectrums. Shrugging, the cybernetic champion ventured into the hangar.

And just beyond the range of Cyborg's sensors, two sets of eyes spied on the

Watchtower. One pair belonged to Mr. Mxyzptlk. They blinked open while the rest of his impish body remained camouflaged against the stars. The other pair of eyes were electronic in nature. They belonged to a robotic drone that hailed from across the universe—in a fiery, fearsome world known as Apokolips. These two sets of eyes then winked at each other like co-conspirators who were about to spring a trap. . . .

Chapter 4
Cy-Burger

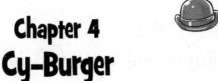

Batman and Superman were examined by futuristic scanners in the Watchtower's medical bay. When the scan was complete, Cyborg frowned.

"The readouts do not show anything out of the ordinary," he said. "Whatever Mxy did to you, guys, must be rooted in some kind of magic. Since I am technology-based, I'm afraid there isn't much I can do to help."

"That's all right," Batman said, patting Cyborg's metallic shoulder. "You tried your hardest, and that's what really counts."

Cyborg gave Batman a sidelong glance and said, "O*kaaay* . . ."

"Just consider yourself lucky you haven't also been affected by the spell," Batman added.

"Likely because Cyborg was up here in space and alone, so there was no one else to swap powers with," Superman concluded.

Suddenly, the Watchtower's trouble alert went off. Sirens echoed throughout the satellite corridors. Overhead lights flashed red. The three Super Heroes ran down the hall to the monitor room, and Cyborg silenced the trouble alert while activating every screen. They displayed various unsettling scenarios around the globe: Gravity still hadn't returned to Metropolis, where Lex Luthor's wig floated off his bald head! Central City was now in the clutches of severe winter and its frozen streets were transformed into a giant ice maze! And Gotham City turned into an overgrown jungle, where a clown-faced Wonder Woman threw pies at a magic lasso-twirling Harley Quinn!

"Great Krypton!" said Batman.

"There's nothing great about this," Superman growled.

"Okay, this is just getting weird!" Cyborg said. "But I *think* I know what's going on."

He opened a hatch in his torso. It resembled a small oven, complete with an orange heating lamp. Cyborg removed two different veggie burgers from inside the warm compartment and said, "I was going to save these for lunch, but this is more important. Because if I'm right, you haven't just switched powers. You've switched personalities, too!"

Batman and Superman traded worried looks. Cyborg held up one of the burgers and said, "I call this one the BBQ Bomb. It has a plant-based patty, fake bacon, onion rings, cheddar, and barbecue glaze, all on a seeded bun."

Cyborg then indicated the second burger. "And this is a Cyborg Classic, which comes with lettuce, tomato, pickles, and secret sauce—a blend of ketchup, mustard, and butterscotch—inside a *seedless* bun."

Superman's stomach rumbled. Normally, he could go days without getting hungry. Batman pointed to a pouch on the Utility

Belt, and Superman opened it, finding a granola bar.

"In case of emergencies," Batman whispered helpfully.

"Now, when Mr. Mxyzptlk zapped you, it first seemed like you had only switched buns," Cyborg explained.

He put the BBQ Bomb in the seedless bun and the Cyborg Classic in the seeded bun.

Cyborg handed the burgers to the heroes and said, "Here you are. See? You're wearing each other's buns!"

"I'm getting uncomfortable with this metaphor," Superman growled.

"But," Cyborg said with emphasis, "it's not just the buns that moved. The condiments in the original burgers—the barbecue glaze and sweet, sweet Cyborg sauce—were stuck on those buns and have now transferred to the patties of their *new* burgers!"

Batman lifted the bun of his burger, and saw barbecue glaze mingling with the lettuce, tomato, and pickles. "In other words," Batman said, "these changes aren't just superficial. The elements inside of each burger—and inside of us—are rubbing off on each other, too."

"Correct!" said Cyborg, who then took a bite of each burger. "And delicious!"

"It also means that these personality shifts could be permanent if we don't reverse them soon," Superman said, his voice sounding more irritable and gravelly than usual.

"Trust me," Cyborg said. "I know a thing or two about different sides sharing the same body. It's never easy—"

KA-BOOM!

Something struck the monitor room from outside, leaving a gaping hole in the wall. The cold vacuum of space soon sucked out all the breathable air, and everything that wasn't bolted down flew outside, too. Cyborg's feet riveted themselves to the floor, and he reached out to grab Superman. Oxygen masks then popped out of another compartment on

Cyborg's body. He and Superman donned them, although Batman no longer needed one.

"Hang on!" Cyborg shouted over the escaping air. "The Watchtower's under attack!"

Chapter 5
Sign of the Apokolips

The pressure soon regulated, and Superman, Batman, and Cyborg took stock of the situation. Lights flickered, alarms blared, and wreckage littered their bombarded headquarters.

"Whatever hit us made Swiss cheese of the Watchtower's force fields!" said Cyborg.

The satellite's back up generators kicked on, and power cycled throughout the base

once more. The monitor room's cracked
screens displayed images again, although
they all broadcast the same thing. At first,
the three Justice Leaguers thought they

were looking at an extreme close-up of the side of a towering mountain. But then that mountain smiled.

"Darkseid!" cried Superman and Batman.

The granite-faced ruler of Apokolips grinned even wider. Batman used his super-vision to peer through the hole in the wall and spotted an entire Apokoliptic armada surrounding their space station. Darkseid's warship was at the forefront of the fleet.

"Ah! So we meet again, *Super Heroes*," Darkseid said with contempt. "You have one minute to surrender—or not. I don't really care. I'm taking over your world either way."

"Three invasions in one morning?" said Batman.

"Mondays really are the worst . . . ," grumbled Superman.

"Fools!" Darkseid said. "There is no coincidence in the cosmos. Only conquest."

"Then this attack is something you've been plotting for a while, isn't it?" Cyborg asked.

"Indeed," said Darkseid. "The obnoxious pest you call Mxyzptlk shared his plan before unleashing it on your world. He was surprisingly wise to first gain my permission—and to attempt no such swap spell with me. If he had, my Omega Beams would have turned that Fifth Dimensional dolt into a mound of ash under a silly hat!"

"But now you're infiltrating Earth while our powers are switched," Batman said.

"And there's nothing *Super-Bat* or *Man-Man* can do about it!" Darkseid gloated.

"Especially considering how your one minute has elapsed. I nobly accept your surrender."

Superman tapped a Utility Belt button. "Who said anything about surrender?" he asked.

Darkseid's eyes bulged as the Batwing streaked out of the Watchtower's hangar. The supersonic craft strafed the Apokoliptic armada, pummeling it with grenades. Superman worked the remote Batwing controls in the Utility Belt, and Batman and Cyborg watched on the monitors as Darkseid's massive warship rattled from the countless blasts. The tyrant's craggy face twisted in anger. "What are you waiting for?" he yelled to his troops. "Fight back, curse you! FIGHT BACK!"

Then Darkseid remembered he was still on camera and feigned calm. "I mean—end transmission," he said.

The signal cut out, and Superman, Batman, and Cyborg raced down a hallway. Along the way, Batman smiled at Superman and said, "A sneak attack, eh? I'm impressed!"

"Just taking a page from your playbook," Superman responded humorlessly.

Reaching the supply room, Cyborg swapped out his old appendages for bigger, more formidable attachments—a sonic disruptor and a pulsar cannon—while Batman helped Superman into one of his bulky Bat-spacesuits.

"This thing weighs a ton," said Superman.

"It won't out there," Batman said. "And it'll keep you safe and warm."

"Oh, I wouldn't worry about the cold—especially with all this firepower!" said Cyborg.

Cyborg activated his upgrades, which illuminated and thrummed. The rocket pack on his back ignited, carrying him through the hangar and into space. Batman flew after him with ease, while Superman brought up the rear as his spacesuit levitated with puffs of compressed air.

Exiting the Watchtower, Cyborg, Batman, and Superman propelled themselves toward Darkseid's fleet. But as they got closer, Cyborg stopped abruptly, and the other two heroes bumped into him.

"Uh, fellas?" Cyborg said nervously. "I think we've got company."

Batman and Superman looked past him and saw thousands of insectlike soldiers swarming out of every vessel from Apokolips. The mass of buzzing, bug-eyed grunts wielded staffs that arced with electric green currents, and they soon surrounded the trio.

"Parademons!" Cyborg shouted. "I don't have a fly-swatter—but I do have *these*!"

He scrambled one Parademon battalion with his sonic disruptor, then scattered another with the pulsar cannon. Following Cyborg's lead, Batman unleashed his heat vision again, chopping off the ends of the Parademons' staffs so they were left holding useless nubs. Superman then catapulted a series of bolas—weighted balls attached to each other by strong ropes—that ensnared the Apokoliptic army.

"Yes!" Cyborg shouted cheerfully. "Even when things get topsy-turvy, the Justice League stays nervy!"

He gave Batman a high five, then turned to Superman. Unfortunately, Superman forgot he no longer had super-strength. When Cyborg's metal palm met with his, the high five sent the Bat-spacesuit spinning.

Superman attempted to regain control by firing more compressed air puffs, but they only spiraled him further out of control. He crashed into Batman, who, in turn, slammed into Cyborg. The collision knocked Cyborg's attachments loose and sent him flying into a new Parademon platoon.

"You guys don't happen to like veggie burgers, do you?" he asked.

The Parademons looked at each other in bewilderment, then dragged Cyborg back to the lead warship. Batman took flight after him, but his new super-strength made him a bit overconfident. Kryptonians were invulnerable to many things—but not to Kryptonite, which powered the Parademons' battle staffs. The weapons sparked and zapped the brash Batman, who fell instantly ill, drifting away from the withdrawing Parademons.

"That . . . felt . . . way worse . . . than I imagined . . . ," he said with a groan.

By the time Superman halted his tailspin and retrieved Batman, it was too late. Darkseid and his minions pointed their fleet at Earth and left the two helpless heroes in their wake.

Mr. Mxyzptlk, still invisible, watched them from afar, giggling with glee. Everything was happening just as he'd hoped—with even more fun yet to come!

Chapter 6
Dark Seid of the Moon

"That could have gone much better," said Superman.

"But it didn't," grumbled Batman.

Superman and Batman's dizziness abated, only to be replaced by guilt. As they floated in silence, they regretted their inability to prevent Cyborg's capture. And to make matters worse, they saw that the Batwing's engine had been gutted by the savage Parademons.

"I'm well enough to fly back to Earth," said Batman. "But you'll burn up on reentry . . ."

"Cooking me like one of Cyborg's burgers," Superman finished grimly. "And you can't face Darkseid alone. The Kryptonite cores of the Parademons' staffs will weaken you again."

"I'll just have to hit them faster—and harder," Batman said, recalling his usual style.

"That's not how it works," said Superman, remembering his own old self. "Take it from me, friend. When you can do things that other people can't, you have to show control, not carelessness."

"Spoken like someone who's never had to strike from the shadows," muttered Batman. "I've always needed to calculate my every move before facing off against much stronger foes. But now is the time for a direct approach. We can't keep pulling our punches."

"Don't take it personally, Bruce," said Superman, holding up his hands in a calming gesture. "I've had a lifetime to learn that lesson. You've only had a few hours."

"Maybe you learned the *wrong* lesson, Clark," Batman replied. "I refuse to fight with one arm tied behind my back—especially when I have a whole new set of resources at my command, instead of a bunch of bat-shaped gadgets I built all by my—"

"*Ahem,*" interrupted a crisp British voice over the spacesuit radio, surprising Superman.

Batman also heard it with his new keen hearing. "Alfred?" he said.

"Got it in one, Master Bruce," Alfred the butler said, loud and clear. "Although, if

I may be so bold, I do seem to recall playing *some* small part in building your arsenal of Bat-gear."

"Er, of course you did, Alfred," Batman said. "I . . . I'm sorry."

The Dark Knight wasn't typically in the habit of apologizing, but doing so brought back that unfamiliar—yet not unpleasant—sense of lightness. In truth, Batman now felt quite embarrassed for needling Superman. And Superman felt angry at what Batman had said, only he did not admit it. This time, the Man of Steel believed it was best to put aside his feelings and focus entirely on the task at hand.

"How bad is it, Alfred?" Superman asked.

"Quite dire, I'm afraid," said Alfred. "The Batcave's radar predicts that Darkseid's forces will reach your upended city in a matter of minutes."

Images from the Batcomputer, TV news cameras, and shaky cell phone footage all appeared on the spacesuit's visor display, courtesy of Alfred. Each showed Darkseid's warships looming over Metropolis. And since the Apokolips armada had been off Earth when Mxyzptlk cast his spells, it was immune to the inverted gravity.

"Might we expect assistance from the rest of the Justice League, Master Bruce?" asked the butler.

"They're all on other missions," Batman explained. "And suffering the same swap situation."

"Perhaps there are some other, *younger* allies I may reach on your behalf?" Alfred hinted.

"Do it, Alfred," Superman said, beating Batman to it.

"Very good, sir," answered Alfred. "Oh, and Master Bruce? Since you no longer have

60

need of your 'bat-shaped gadgets,' perhaps
Superman might avail himself of them?"

"That's a great idea, Alfred!" Batman said.
"Thank you for suggesting it!"

Hearing the unexpected cheer in Batman's voice—a gloomy man Alfred had helped raise since he was a gloomy boy—gave the butler pause. When he finally got over his shock, he said, "My, my, *this* is a welcome change!"

As Batman made a mental note to say "sorry" and "thank you" more often, Superman saw one of Cyborg's veggie burgers float by. It had become crystallized with ice, but Superman could still see the bite Cyborg had taken out of it, which made the burger look like a crescent. An idea began to form in Superman's head—a crafty, cunning idea worthy of Batman himself.

"I need a lift to the moon," Superman said curtly. "And step on it."

"Safe travels, sirs," Alfred said over the communicator.

Batman looped his strong arms around Superman, then zoomed away. En route, Superman shared the plan he'd just devised, and Batman once again grew impressed with his friend—then worried. Superman's plan would be difficult, if not downright impossible.

Yet that wasn't what worried Batman. It was the distant, cold way in which Superman detailed the steps. Something about it seemed

familiar to Batman. He soon realized why—
it was the way he himself often spoke, up
until this very morning. Had Cyborg been
right with his veggie burger comparison?
Had Batman's dark, complex barbecue
taste somehow tainted Superman's brighter,
fresher flavor? The question chilled the
Caped Crusader more than the coldest
reaches of space.

They reached the moon in a matter of
seconds, which came as a great relief to the
heroes. Even though neither one had said
it out loud, the idea of Batman carrying
Superman felt very, very weird to both of
them. Circling around to the moon's far side,
they located the first element of Superman's
subversive strategy: Batman's lunar armory.
Batman built the fortress as a back up bunker,

in case his Batcave—and all the advanced technology within it—should ever be discovered or destroyed by Super-Villains.

Superman and Batman passed through an airlock, then entered the armory. The artificial gravity and atmosphere generators kicked on, and Superman removed his helmet. He inhaled a deep breath of fresh oxygen, then marveled at Batman's hidden array of groundbreaking gadgets.

"This'll do," Superman said with a sly smirk.

"I'm glad to hear that," said Batman. "I'm off to take care of my part of the plan. Wish me luck!"

"I don't believe in luck," Superman said brusquely. "Not anymore."

Batman shook his head in dismay and turned to leave, while Superman walked

down an aisle lined with different-colored Batsuits—a white uniform for arctic missions, an aquamarine one for underwater adventures, and more. He stopped by a uniform that was displayed at the end of the aisle. His devious grin widened, as he marveled at the coal-black suit of tactical armor complete with mechanized wings, spiked gauntlets, and glowing red piping that matched the bat insignia on the chest and the helmet visor. Superman read the nearby sign. "So this is the most powerful Batsuit of all," he said. This is the Hel—"

Batman swooped back and frantically covered the rest of the sign. "To be honest, I was kind of in a bad place when I named this suit," he said with an awkward smile. "And maybe it's just your incredibly polite, midwestern manners rubbing off on me, but how about we call it something a tad friendlier?"

Superman stepped inside the armor. "Fine," he said. We'll call it . . . the *Heck*-Batsuit!"

Chapter 7
What the Heck

As soon as Robin and Batgirl's motorcycles crossed Metropolis's city limits, they lifted off the asphalt as if the tires were filled with helium. Any other bikers would be shocked, but these two sidekicks, whose faces were covered by their driving helmets, had been trained by Batman to always expect the unexpected. They fired their grappling hooks. The lines wrapped around a mailbox, and the two young heroes towed their bikes to the ground, then removed their helmets—only it was Batgirl under Robin's helmet and Robin under Batgirl's! Like Superman and Batman, these two had been swapped, too.

"It took me one extra second to find the grappling hook in your Utility Belt," Batgirl said. "That might mean the difference between life and death. You should organize your stuff better."

"Yeah, yeah," Robin replied with a roll of his eyes.

A shadow eclipsed them. They looked up and saw Darkseid's warship descending through the cloudless sky. Scores of Parademons spread out before it, an advance scout sweeping for any potential obstacles to their takeover.

"Ol' Alfred wasn't kidding when he said that thing was huge!" Robin said in awe.

Batgirl hurled a Batarang, and Robin followed up by lobbing handfuls of pellets. The miniature smoke bombs detonated around the swarm of incoming Parademons, producing a smokescreen that disoriented them—and allowed Batgirl's Batarang to circle around for its return trip. It came back with a vengeance, bonking the unsuspecting Parademons' heads.

Because both teens were accomplished acrobats and martial artists, they barely noticed that their abilities had switched along with their wardrobes. So they didn't let up, peppering the Parademons with more smoke pellets, Batarangs . . . and Batgirl's cell phone.

"Hey!" she cried. "I just got that repaired after Killer Croc stepped on it!"

"Oops!" said Robin. "You keep your phone in the same place I keep my putty bombs!"

Two zigzagging laser beams struck the ground in front of them. Batgirl and Robin flew into the air, landing several feet away, rolling with the impact, as Batman had taught them.

Darkseid descended slowly on a hovering platform, his hands clasped behind his back, his eyes still glowing from the Omega Beams they'd just projected. Cyborg had been plugged into the front of the platform, where power-dampeners—devices that steal energy—drained him. He was very weak. The stone-skinned ruler of Apokolips curled his lip in distaste at Robin and Batgirl.

"Costumed children," he said with a sneer. "Is this the best defense your world has to offer?"

HONK-HONK!

Darkseid turned just in time to see the Batmobile. Two grappling hook lines swung the Caped Crusader's car like a wrecking ball directly toward him.

"Glorious Godfrey!" Darkseid bellowed.

He leapt out of the way and landed face-first in the dirt. And after Darkseid had cleared the grit from his eyes, he saw the Heck-Batsuit standing before him, the two grappling hook lines retracting into its wrists, its splayed wings backlit by the sun. Superman's voice spoke from inside the armor, sounding more and more like Batman's as he said, "You should look both ways before crossing the road—*and crossing me.*"

"Ah, the Superman who became the Man-Man has now become the Bat-Man-Man," Darkseid taunted.

Robin and Batgirl exchanged a perplexed look, then went back to pelting Parademons.

Darkseid's eyes flared red and emitted two more Omega Beams. Superman brought the Heck-Batsuit's wings forward, and they shielded him from the brunt of the beams. He flapped the smoldering wings and rose into the air. Reaching a height of one hundred feet, Superman dove headlong at his enemy. The Heck-Batsuit's fists connected with Darkseid's, producing a resounding shock wave that knocked everyone to the ground.

Superman was the first to recover as the Heck-Batsuit suit once again absorbed the worst of the punishment. He helped Robin and Batgirl to their feet.

"Thanks, Superman," said Robin.

"Uh, that *is* Superman in there, isn't it?" Batgirl asked.

"More or less," said Superman.

Batgirl watched Darkseid stride toward them. "What now?" she asked. "Darkseid doesn't have a scratch on him!"

"If Batman were here, he'd know what to do," Robin said.

"Batman *is* here," Superman insisted. "More or less."

The display inside the Heck-Batsuit's helmet filled with streams of code. Superman prepared himself for round two. He cracked his knuckles, saying, "As a farmboy in Kansas, I didn't have as many toys as Batman did when he was growing up. But now I want to play with them—*all of them.*"

A humongous high-tech mechanical robot lowered between Darkseid and Superman on its sizable set of boot jets, whirring its gears and readying its weapons. A hatch

opened on its back, and Superman stepped inside. Encased within the levitating mech, he plugged his Heck-Batsuit hands and feet into the larger contraption's limbs. Now Superman was in a suit inside another suit!

"I'm glad this thing's on our side!" Batgirl said as she and Robin climbed onto its back.

"Yes, challenge me, not-so-Superman," said Darkseid. "Face your greatest fear!"

"I am fear," said Superman in his most convincing Batman voice.

The Parademons flanked Darkseid as he rushed toward the Super Heroes, and the Superman-controlled robot barreled toward the Super-Villains. Both sides collided in the middle of Metropolis, kicking off an epic rumble that shook the entire city!

And the invisible Mr. Mxyzptlk, who had a front-row seat to the fighting, clapped his little hands and cheered, "Now, *this* is what I call fun!"

Chapter 8
Goodness and Darkness

Superman's directions had been quite clear: *Hang a left at Oa, then go past New Genesis. Slow down and pay attention. If you reach the Source Wall, you've gone too far.* Batman finally arrived at Darkseid's deep-space planet, Apokolips, and entered its polluted atmosphere. Once he passed through the thick smog layer, the Dark Knight took in the world's grim landscape. Yet he remained upbeat in spite

of the blazing firepits and Darkseid statues as tall as skyscrapers.

"Look! Up in the sky! It's a bat! It's a Wayne! No, it's Super Stand-In!" Batman joked to no one in particular, before his face soured in disgust. "Since when did the Dark Knight get so cheerful? I'd better hurry, before this horrible condition worsens!"

He touched down at what he could only assume was the capital of Apokolips, given the volcano that had been carved to resemble Darkseid's head. Lava poured from the mouth like red-hot bile, and a caped, stocky figure appeared silhouetted by its glow.

"Pardon me," said Batman, who was now back in the mindset of an optimistic, super powerful alien raised by a kindly Kansas couple. "Would you mind pointing me toward Darkseid's vault?"

The figure stepped forward, revealing a shock of bone-white hair and wild eyes. Her crimson lips leered, making even more wrinkles appear on her shriveled, heat-baked face. Batman gasped, recognizing Granny Goodness, who trained all of Apokolips's wildest warriors.

"Certainly," Granny said warmly. "After all, I'm not just Darkseid's drill sergeant. I'm also head of the Apokolips hospitality committee! Here, I even have a welcome gift for you. . . ."

She reached under her cloak and pulled out a big, heavy club. Granny swung the weapon with unexpected speed!

The sucker punch did not hurt Batman, but it sent him somersaulting into a pool of magma. Fortunately, his Kryptonian garb was wrinkle-free *and* lava-proof, and Batman barely even felt Granny Goodness's surprise attack. In the past, he would have retreated to think up a way to outwit his enemy. But now he could take the fight straight to her.

As Batman rose unharmed from the lava, molten rock sliding off him in sizzling drops, Granny grew nervous and said, "Y-you wouldn't hurt a sweet old lady, would you, now?"

"Of course not," Batman replied. "But you're not sweet!"

He grabbed Granny Goodness's cloak and swung her over his head again and again. The centrifugal force was so strong, Granny's dentures slipped out of her mouth!

"Muh teef!" Granny garbled.

When Batman finally released her, she sailed over Apokolips and lodged into one of the giant Darkseid statues. Her head jutted out of where Darkseid's carved face had been, while her legs dangled from the back of the statue's skull. The ridiculous sight reminded Batman of those plywood cutouts found at carnivals, where people put their faces through holes so they look like they're part of the caricatured bodies painted on the front. Why, he used to love seeing those at the Smallville county fair every—

"Wait a minute!" Batman exclaimed. "That's one of Superman's memories, not mine! This switcheroo is getting stranger by the second. . . ."

The clarity of Superman's childhood memory made Batman think of another

thing that belonged to Superman—
X-ray vision. Batman watched in wonder
as the solid walls of the Apokolips
capital became transparent. He scanned
the structure, discovering several of
Darkseid's henchmen enjoying private
moments—Desaad taking a bubble
bath, Steppenwolf using his axe to cut
a sandwich in half, Mantis rubbing his
appendages together to make music—but
no vault.

On a hunch, Batman looked straight
down. About one mile below, at the base
of a vast volcanic fire pit, he saw an
immense locked door. Yet Batman couldn't
see through that door, meaning the entire
vault was forged of the one material that
his X-rays could not penetrate. . . .

"Solid lead," he said. "Something valuable must be hidden inside."

Batman wrapped his red cape around his body, then began to spin on the tips of his toes. Like a human drill, he bored through the bedrock, burrowing past layer after layer of strata until he reached the base of the pit. His heat vision did the rest, shearing the leaden door off its hinges. It fell forward with a *CLANG*, and Batman stepped over it to enter Darkseid's vault. Riches from across the multiverse lined the walls: amethysts from Gemworld, prototype artillery belonging to the Weaponers of Qward, deactivated Green Lantern batteries, and more. But all of those paled in comparison to the one, true treasure—a black diamond that throbbed with foul energy.

"So Batman, you have found the Heart of Darkness," said a savage voice.

Batman turned around, caught off guard. Superman was right—his powers really *had* made Batman careless. If he'd been in his right mind, Batman never would have entered a room without determining who else might be lurking within. But now he found himself face to face with Kalibak, the son of Darkseid. Kalibak's hulking size meant he was a threat to be reckoned with. Yet Batman also recognized a childlike innocence in the brute's eyes.

"I will not let you take the source of my father's power," Kalibak continued. "He anticipated such treachery and left me here to guard it, rather than join in his crushing invasion of your pathetic planet. That, *and*

I accidentally scratched my dad's warship, so he grounded me."

"I once had to do the same thing when Robin took my Batcopter for a joyride," admitted Batman. "But he's a good kid, and you seem like one, too, Kalibak. So, let's say we skip the slugfest and you let me have what I came here for."

"Oh, I'll let you have it!" said Kalibak.

He tackled Batman, their bodies slamming into the wall and making the firepit shake. Batman pushed back, and the two fighters crashed into the opposite wall, summoning another quake.

"You also seem like a fine fellow—far kinder than my father," Kalibak said through gritted teeth. "But I am supposed to complete my chores before bedtime . . . and defeating someone with Superman's might is at the top of my list!"

Batman and Kalibak traded blows, their tremendous slobber-knocker of a battle jolting the very foundations of Apokolips— and triggering a cave-in that buried them both under an avalanche of rubble!

Chapter 9
Dropping the BOOM

The Heck-Batsuit had seen better days. It was missing one wing, from when Darkseid had pried Superman out of the larger mech, and sparks shot from its frayed circuits. Darkseid held up Superman with one hand, although the mighty lord of Apokolips looked worse for wear as well. One of his eyes had swollen shut, meaning Darkseid could now only fire one Omega Beam at a time. All around the two run-down fighters, weightless wreckage cluttered the air.

"Do you . . . yield?" Darkseid asked, out of breath.

Superman, who was also winded, said, "Super Heroes . . . never . . . quit."

"Your allies . . . would seem to indicate . . . otherwise," Darkseid goaded.

He pointed to Batgirl and Robin. The Parademons, who greatly outnumbered the valiant teens, had trussed them in their own Batropes and tossed them next to Cyborg, who was still out of energy.

"Those kids have more heart than you ever will, Darkseid," said Superman. "It figures that you'd wait to attack when all of our abilities are swapped, rather than face us in a fair fight."

"Fair?" said Darkseid. "Where I come from, there is no such thing as 'fair'—except our annual Pain and Misery Fair, of course. But, honestly, I doubt that festival is what you were referring to."

Superman smirked behind his battered helmet. "You'll never know, you big—"

BOOOOOM!

Pure cosmic force thundered through the city of Metropolis, throwing Superman and Darkseid apart. When they staggered to their feet and looked up, a Boom Tube—a teleport tunnel connecting one end of the universe to another—materialized. Wind and light rushed out, followed by Batman, who clutched a certain black diamond.

"My Heart of Darkness!" Darkseid cried. "But . . . but Kalibak guarded that with his

life! If Super-Bat possesses it, then this can only mean you have destroyed my favorite son. I mean, except for Orion. And Mr. Miracle, too, I guess. Little Death Spawn has issues, though."

"Wait for me!" yelled a deep voice from inside the glowing tunnel.

Kalibak emerged and ran eagerly to Batman's side. "Anything else I can do to help my new best pal? On top of opening a Boom Tube to Earth, that is!"

"*What?*" Darkseid shouted, slapping his sloped forehead. "My own offspring aiding Batman? Surely my boy has been brainwashed!"

"There was no mind control, Darkseid," said Batman. "Only chitchat. When we were buried under tons of fallen rock, I convinced

Kalibak that we'd need to work together if either one of us was to ever escape. Anyway, as we were heaving boulders, we got to talking, and it turned out—"

"We have a lot in common!" Kalibak chimed in. "We both live in scary cities, we both like caves, we both wish we could hug our dads . . . you know, stuff like that."

"In my eons-long life, I have never been more deceived," Darkseid muttered.

"That was the plan," Batman said. "Well, except Kalibak becoming my new sidekick."

"And you deceived yourself, Darkseid, when you assumed our swapped powers would make us power*less*," Superman said as he limped over to Batman. "Superpowers or no superpowers, we now hold the one thing capable of stopping you. No wonder you never show any heart—you keep it locked away in a vault."

"Actually, Superman, you *did* get one power from me," said Batman. "Sneakiness."

He slapped his friend on the back, knocking the other wing off the Heck-Batsuit suit.

"I'll fix that!" Kalibak volunteered.

"No, traitor, I'll *fix* you!" Darkseid shouted.

Enraged, Darkseid Omega-blasted his son, knocking him out. He then barreled toward his adversaries, a new beam charging in his unswollen eye. But Superman and Batman had spent enough time in each other's boots to know what to do next. They split up, moving in tandem, as they always had—only in a whole new way.

Rather than take on Darkseid head-to-head, Superman slipped behind him. And rather than strike from the shadows, Batman attacked Darkseid directly. The Caped Crusader and Darkseid grappled against each other with all the brawn they could muster, but neither budged. It was a total standstill. Darkseid tilted his head down, about to unleash his Omega Beam.

And that was when Superman clambered onto his nemesis's neck and held the Heart of Darkness—which he'd furtively grabbed

from Batman—over Darkseid's open eye. Darkseid tried to shake off Superman, but Batman held him steady and said, "Go ahead, Darkseid. You can blast me. . . ."

"But you'll destroy the source of your own power in the process," Superman finished.

"Impossible!" Darkseid snarled. "You lie!"

"No, I don't," said Batman. "Not anymore."

"*I* may have started, though," Superman said. "Want to see if I'm telling the truth?"

Darkseid seethed. The Omega Beam swelled behind his glowering eye, growing and growing and growing, until . . . it extinguished. Superman felt the heat fade from Darkseid's face, while Batman felt the villain's body go slack. Despite the odds, despite their strange swapped situation, they had defeated Darkseid.

"Name your terms," said Darkseid sullenly.

"The Heart of Darkness will be yours again, *if* your army vacates Earth," Batman said.

"And *if* you use your diamond to return our world to normal," said Superman.

Darkseid threw back his head and laughed bitterly. "Darkseid is all-powerful, but not *that* all-powerful!" he said. "My Heart of Darkness only contains enough energy to repair this city . . . or the two of you. Now decide!"

Superman and Batman looked at each other in shock. Would their mismatched powers and personalities be permanent? What that meant for them and the planet they'd sworn to protect, neither champion could say. But in the end, there was never really any choice to make.

"Fix the city," Superman grumbled.

"We'll figure out another way to fix ourselves," said Batman. "I hope."

Darkseid nodded solemnly, then focused on the diamond as Superman set it in his hand. The Heart of Darkness illuminated from within, casting a bright light across all of Metropolis. A moment later, things began to change once again. Clouds and hot-air balloons rose into the sky. Lawn furniture and empty school buses came gently back down to Earth. And, true to their bargain, Darkseid's Parademons released Batgirl and

Robin from their bonds, then retreated on buzzing wings back to their ships. The two teens helped a grateful Cyborg out of his power-dampeners. His energy levels started to rise, although all three heroes were still pretty weak.

Darkseid said, "Does this conclude our negotiation?"

Superman and Batman both nodded. "Yes," they said.

"No!" squealed a squeaky voice from nearby. "No! No! NO!"

Chapter 10
Double Double-Crossed

Mr. Mxyzptlk made himself visible. He was boiling with anger.

"You!" he yelled pointing at Batman, Superman, and Darkseid. "You don't get to ruin my fun! The only one who says playtime is over—and who can un-swap anybody—is me! And I won't *ever* do that!"

"Fine," Superman said.

"I'm cool with that, too," said Batman.

"Wh-wh-what?" Mxyzptlk stammered in disbelief.

"We just realized we *don't want* to go back to the way we were," Superman explained.

"Sure, I never once thought I needed superpowers," Batman added. "I mean, not to brag, but I was already pretty good at fighting crime *before* I could fly or shoot eye-lasers or whatever. Only now . . . well, I guess

you could say these abilities have grown on me."

"What he said," seconded a super-serious Superman. "At first I *did* want my abilities back, desperately, to help the people who have come to depend upon me. But now that I've gotten my hands on bat-themed technology? You can keep the superpowers—they're a small price to pay for getting to explore my *darker* side."

"That's darker *seid*," Darkseid interjected.

"*Darker* side?" spluttered the Fifth Dimension imp. "You don't have a darker side!"

"Keep telling yourself that, Mxyzptlk," Superman said, before shifting into his Batman voice. *"But I've already devised twenty-seven ways to defeat you."*

"Twenty-seven, you say?" asked Mxyzptlk, nervously tugging at his collar.

"Now it's twenty-eight," Superman corrected. *"All without powers. I just need a big feather, a pair of old socks, and one economy-sized jar of mayonnaise."*

Cyborg perked up and said, "What is he going to do with all of those?"

"You don't want to know," Robin and Batgirl answered in unison.

"Uh, Superman," Batman began. "Maybe you should relax. And quit impersonating me."

"I'm not," Superman rasped.

"You just did!" Batman said.

"What are you talking about?"

"There you go again! Stop it! Seriously!"

"I can't help myself."

Darkseid, Cyborg, Batgirl, and Robin's eyes ping-ponged between the two Super

Heroes as they continued arguing. The constant quibbling so irritated Mr. Mxyzptlk that he pulled his bowler hat down over his ears and screeched, "QUIET!"

Everything in Metropolis went silent— including Kalibak's snoring. Mxyzptlk paced the air, muttering, "This silly swap was supposed to be fun, but you're no fun at all! I'm switching you back—but *only* you two—whether you want it or not— just to stop your bickering!"

He wiggled his fingers, struck Superman and Batman with a second strobe of light, and disappeared with a loud *POP.* When the spots faded from everyone's eyes, they saw that Batman and Superman were back in their own outfits—and back to their old selves . . . or were they?

"I can't believe that worked," Superman said, then cracked up. "Sorry, I couldn't resist!"

"Ha ha," Batman said sarcastically. "But I *can* believe it. It was a good plan."

"You *arranged* that argument?" Darkseid asked.

"Yes, we did. Mxyzptlk doesn't like bad attitudes spoiling his 'fun,'" Superman explained.

"And since we know that he delights in doing the opposite of what others want, we said we didn't need our powers back—only to wind up with the very outcome we truly desired," finished Batman.

"Wow! Holy reverse psychology!" Batgirl exclaimed, startling everyone.

"I guess the rest of us are still swapped," said a disappointed Robin. "I don't want to complain, but . . . You know . . ."

"I've got my original programming, so to speak," Cyborg corrected. "And there must be others who have remained themselves and can help us reverse the rest of Mxyzptlk's spell . . . somehow."

"Yeah, good luck with all of that," Darkseid deadpanned. He nudged the snoozing Kalibak with his boot, rousing him. "Come, whelp. We return now to the stinking, scalding embrace of our home world . . . which seems absolutely sane compared to this mixed-up mudball."

Darkseid marched over to the Boom Tube, then stopped short. He saw that his son hadn't left the Batman's side. Averting his eyes, Kalibak said, "Father, I would prefer to remain here and learn from your enemies—and my new friends. Perhaps then I will be less of a disappointment to you."

Batman and Kalibak shared a private nod. "So be it," said Darkseid. "If this entire

experience has taught me anything, it is to expect the unexpected. Besides, little Death Spawn could probably benefit from my undivided attention for a few weeks."

No sooner did Darkseid enter the Boom Tube than it collapsed into itself and vanished. Superman surveyed the damage left in his wake. "That's the end of one headache," he said.

"Although we still have our Mxyzptlk problem," Batman replied.

Still sensing the fading influence of Batman within him, Superman said, "We need to form a strike force with members who have experienced this power swap."

"I'm in," said Batman. "And that means my partners are in, too—including Kalibak."

"Holy recruitment drive!" Batgirl blurted.

"Dang it, this is getting out of hand!" said Robin.

Superman put a reassuring hand on Robin's shoulder and said, "Don't worry. We won't stop until you're un-swapped."

An overjoyed Kalibak jumped up and down with glee, saying, "I promise I won't let down my pal, Batman, or —"

In his excitement, Kalibak almost accidentally stomped on the same kitten that Superman had rescued—only for Batman to scoop her up just in time. She meowed and gave the Dark Knight an appreciative lick on the cheek.

"Maybe things haven't gone back to *exactly* the way they were," Superman said, smiling.

"Speaking of that," Batman replied. "I just want to say . . . *I'm sorry*."

Batgirl and Robin did a double take at Batman's unexpected apology. The Dark Knight had more to say, though. He set the kitten down on the ground, where she rubbed against his boots, then he faced Superman. "Back when we were in space, I made some comments about you and your abilities that I now regret," he said. "That was no way to talk to a friend."

"A strong friendship doesn't mean that the friends never fight," Superman said, his smile widening. "It means they forgive each other and move on."

Batman's square jaw dropped. "My . . . my father used to tell me that," he whispered.

"I know," said the Man of Steel. "I heard it in your memories. Your parents were fine people."

"Thank you," Batman said, feeling his chest swell. "So were yours."

Superman and Batman shook hands, then regarded the heroes—and Darkseid's deputized son—assembled on this corner of Metropolis. "Since many of our teammates and their towns need our help, we're splitting into two groups," Batman told them. "Batgirl and Kalibak are taking Gotham with me."

"And I will join Cyborg and Robin in Central City," said Superman. "It's time for all of us to go up, up, and away!"

Following the World's Finest Heroes' orders, Cyborg picked up Robin in his robotic arms and blasted off with his rocket pack, alongside Superman. At the same time, Batgirl and Kalibak strapped themselves into the back of the Batmobile, while Batman sat in the driver's seat. He buckled his seat belt, turned on the ignition, and stepped on the gas—but his foot didn't reach the pedal. Realizing Superman had adjusted the seat, Batman scooted it forward. Batgirl and Kalibak giggled behind him.

"I'm just as tall as Superman!" Batman said defensively. "If you count my bat-ears."

Kalibak patted Batman's shoulder. "My father wears lifts in his boots, too," he said kindly.

"No one in the League can ever hear about this!" barked Batman. *Or else.*

The back seat suddenly went *very* quiet, and the engine roared to life. The Batmobile sped off in one direction and Superman's squad flew in the other. The sun set over Metropolis, and Superman looked at the darkening horizon. The last traces of Batman's personality told him that the coming night would be difficult and dangerous. At the same time, Batman felt Superman's lingering influence tell him they would all get through the night by working together—and that the

following morning would bring the promise of a brighter tomorrow.

In the sky and on the ground, the two Super Heroes smiled to themselves, thinking the same thing at the same time: change can be scary . . . but it can also be good.